For Charlie and Leo with lots of love ~ J C
To my parents ~ M M

LITTLE TIGER PRESS LTD,
an imprint of the Little Tiger Group
1 Coda Studios,
189 Munster Road,
London SW6 6AW
www.littletiger.co.uk

First published in Great Britain 2018

Text copyright © Josephine Collins 2018
Illustrations copyright © Marisa Morea 2018
Josephine Collins and Marisa Morea have asserted their
rights to be identified as the author and illustrator of this
work under the Copyright, Designs and Patents Act, 1988
A CIP catalogue record for this book is
available from the British Library
All rights reserved

ISBN 978-1-78881-005-0
LTP/1400/2178/0318
Printed in China
2 4 6 8 10 9 7 5 3 1

FAIRYTALE CLASSICS

Hansel and Gretel

Josephine Collins   Marisa Morea

LITTLE TIGER

LONDON

Hansel and Gretel lived in a teeny tiny house at the edge of a great forest with their father and stepmother. Their father was a woodcutter, but he was so poor that he didn't even have enough money for food.

"How will we feed the children?" he moaned.
He was a good man and he didn't know that
their stepmother had a plan. A nasty plan . . .

"Husband, we must take the children into the forest and leave them there. Then we can be rid of them!" she said.

"We can't!" spluttered the woodcutter, horrified. But his wife was determined to have her way.

She's such a meany!

Don't worry! I know what to do!

Late that night, as everyone slept, Hansel crept outside. He filled his pockets with pebbles that sparkled like silver coins in the moonlight.

The next morning, the family set off. Clever Hansel dropped the shiny pebbles along the path as they went.

When they reached the middle of the forest, their stepmother announced: "Your father and I are off to chop wood. You stay here."

We'll be back later.

But they didn't come back.

"I'm scared, Hansel!" cried Gretel.

But Hansel knew what to do.

When the moon came up, he took his
little sister by the hand and they
followed the glistening trail of pebbles
all the way home.

Their father was delighted to see them,
but their stepmother said angrily:
"You lazybones! Why did you
sleep so long in the woods?"

That night, she nagged her husband. "We must take them even deeper into the forest!"

And this time, when Hansel got up to collect pebbles, his stepmother had locked the door shut.

The following day, as they set out, Hansel knew what to expect. He made a trail of crumbs from the tiny piece of bread he had been given for breakfast.

"Sit tight, you two!" ordered their stepmother, once they reached the deepest, darkest part of the forest. "We're off to . . . er . . . chop . . . *more* wood! We'll be back later!"

But by nightfall, no one had come for them.

"Don't worry," said Hansel. "We'll follow the trail home!"

Oh, we forgot about the birds!

But the children could not find a single crumb!

They walked for a night and a day
until they were hopelessly lost.
    "I can't go on! I'm so tired and
so hungry," sighed Gretel.

Just then, Hansel spotted
a little house ahead . . .

It was made entirely from gingerbread, sweets and cakes!

The children could not believe their eyes! They ran forwards, and grabbed delicious handfuls of sweet treats.

As they munched happily, an old woman poked her head round the door. "Come inside and stay with me, my dears!" she smiled.

No sooner had the children entered the house, than they realised they had been tricked . . .
The old woman was really a **witch**!

She locked up Hansel, and forced
Gretel to clean and cook.

"You must cook for your brother," she cackled.
"He looks so tasty, I think one day I shall eat him!"
Gretel was terrified.

Every day, the witch
checked to see if Hansel
was ready to eat.

And every day,
clever Hansel fooled the witch.
He knew she couldn't see well, so he held
out a bone instead of his finger.

The witch was very puzzled that Hansel stayed so thin.

"I won't wait any longer!" she snapped. "I'm eating him now! Gretel, light the oven!"

"It won't light," said Gretel.

"Stupid goose!" snarled the witch. And she stuck her head inside the oven to light the flame.

Gretel saw her chance. With all her might, she pushed the witch's bottom!

Take that, you nasty witch!

The witch tumbled into the oven and that was the end of her!

"You've saved us," cried Hansel, as Gretel quickly freed him from the cage.

Now that the children were free to explore the witch's house, they discovered hidden gold and sparkling jewels!

Laughing happily, they filled up their pockets and set off home.

When they arrived, their father hugged them tight.
He had never forgiven himself for leaving the children.
Thankfully their wicked stepmother had left long ago.
From that day on, the woodcutter and his
beloved children were richer than they ever could
have dreamt and never went hungry again.